Animal Escapes

Written by
John Townsend

A Quick Getaway

Small animals have a big problem. They are good to eat!

It can be scary when you are small and tasty. Bigger animals always want to eat you. That means you have to be good at

- hiding,
- moving fast, and
- surprises.

If you can do something amazing, you might surprise a predator. Then you could make a quick getaway.

Some small animals have amazing ways to escape from big jaws …

A Spider Life-line

A juicy spider wants to escape from hungry mouths. How about a life-line for a quick getaway?

If a spider needs to escape, it lets out a strand of silk. As the wind catches it, the spider just 'flies' away.

Some spiders even travel across oceans like this. It is called *ballooning*. It's a great way to lift yourself out of danger!

Octopus Escape

An octopus has no bones. That makes it soft and easy to swallow.

Many fish hunt for octopus. So this sea animal has a few tricks to help it escape:

1. Squirting water from its body to make it shoot off at full speed – like a jet.

2. Squashing into a narrow shape (there are no bones to worry about), so it can squeeze through tiny gaps in rocks.

3. Shape-shifting to look like something else.

Another octopus trick … What do you do if a shark is after you? Easy – just disappear!

A quick squirt of ink does the trick. The octopus can escape behind the 'smoke-screen'.

An octopus pumps out an ink cloud so it can sneak away safely.

Did you know that the mimic octopus can change colour and shape to look just like a deadly fish or sea snake? Anything chasing it will quickly turn and swim off fast!

Lizard Tricks

A lizard can be a tasty snack for many animals.

How can a lizard get away if jaws clamp on its tail? Simple – leave the tail behind. Then it can run off.

Many lizards can shed their tails like this if they have to. They just grow a new tail.

Many animals think the tiny horned lizard will make a great dinner. But just as they go to take a bite, the little reptile puffs up to twice its normal size.

Who wants to eat a spiny balloon?

Then comes the next trick. It shoots blood from its eyes. As a predator gulps with surprise, the horned lizard runs off (maybe with a smile!).

Lizard Superpowers

A basilisk lizard can get away fast. But it does more than dash off. It can run on water.

Nothing chasing it will catch it then!

This lizard traps air under its feet. This keeps it on top of the water.

It has to keep running fast or it will sink.

A gecko lizard can escape by running up walls, windows and even across ceilings.

How?

It has special foot suction. Tiny grooves, pads and hairs on its toes can stick to any surface.

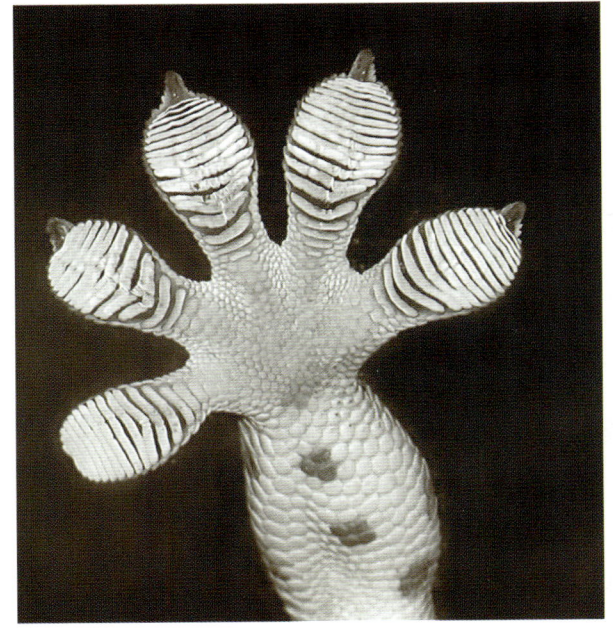

Acting Dead

Some animals can't escape in a hurry if a predator is about to strike. There seems no way out. The only escape is to pretend to be dead!

This opossum acts as if it's dead to stop being eaten. It flops over with its eyes and mouth open. Then it leaks a smelly liquid from its bottom.

It stays like that till the danger has gone.

The hognose snake flips on its back with its mouth wide open. It stays perfectly still. Then it makes a foul smell like rotting flesh.

Nothing will want to eat it now.

Making a Stink

A hungry bear may think a skunk looks tasty.

If a skunk can't run away, it just turns and lifts its tail.

Then it sprays a smelly liquid from its bottom.

A stinky blast of oily mist from under a skunk's bushy tail will make any bear think twice.

While the bear chokes from the foul smell, the skunk can run off safely.

Super-Spit

Even a deadly cobra has a predator. A mongoose loves to eat snakes!

It will run around the cobra and tease it first.

There is no escape for the snake, so what does it do?

The spitting cobra has a great aim. It raises its head and shoots out blinding venom.

Once the cobra has sprayed its enemy's eyes, it can escape. Or it might choose to eat it instead!

Gas Attack

If you are a crawling insect just 3 centimetres long, life can be risky. Everything wants to eat you. If you are a millipede, what can you do to stop getting eaten?

The pink dragon millipede lives in Thailand. It is bright pink and smells of almonds. That's because it fires out a deadly gas if something tries to eat it.

That's a great way to escape without needing to run!